Dear Parents and Educators,

Welcome to Penguin Young Readers! As parents and educators, you know that each child develops at his or her own pace—in terms of speech, critical thinking, and, of course, reading. Penguin Young Readers recognizes this fact. As a result, each Penguin Young Readers book is assigned a traditional easy-to-read level (1–4) as well as a Guided Reading Level (A–P). Both of these systems will help you choose the right book for your child. Please refer to the back of each book for specific leveling information. Penguin Young Readers features esteemed authors and illustrators, stories about favorite characters, fascinating nonfiction, and more!

Strawberry Shortcake™
A Picnic Adventure

LEVEL **2**

GUIDED READING LEVEL **G**

This book is perfect for a **Progressing Reader** who:
- can figure out unknown words by using picture and context clues;
- can recognize beginning, middle, and ending sounds;
- can make and confirm predictions about what will happen in the text; and
- can distinguish between fiction and nonfiction.

Here are some **activities** you can do during and after reading this book:
- Make Connections: In this story, Strawberry Shortcake and her friends go on a picnic. They pack a yummy lunch, a map, and a camera. What would you pack for a picnic with your friends?
- Problem/Solution: The problem in this story is that the map blows away when the girls are at the waterfall. They are afraid they are lost, but they find a solution at last! Discuss how the girls solve their problem and find their way back to the café.

Remember, sharing the love of reading with a child is the best gift you can give!

—Bonnie Bader, EdM
  Penguin Young Readers program

*Penguin Young Readers are leveled by independent reviewers applying the standards developed by Irene Fountas and Gay Su Pinnell in *Matching Books to Readers: Using Leveled Books in Guided Reading*, Heinemann, 1999.

Penguin Young Readers
Published by the Penguin Group
Penguin Group (USA) Inc., 375 Hudson Street, New York, New York 10014, USA
Penguin Group (Canada), 90 Eglinton Avenue East, Suite 700, Toronto, Ontario M4P 2Y3, Canada
(a division of Pearson Penguin Canada Inc.)
Penguin Books Ltd., 80 Strand, London WC2R 0RL, England
Penguin Group Ireland, 25 St. Stephen's Green, Dublin 2, Ireland (a division of Penguin Books Ltd.)
Penguin Group (Australia), 250 Camberwell Road, Camberwell, Victoria 3124, Australia
(a division of Pearson Australia Group Pty. Ltd.)
Penguin Books India Pvt. Ltd., 11 Community Centre, Panchsheel Park, New Delhi—110 017, India
Penguin Group (NZ), 67 Apollo Drive, Rosedale, Auckland 0632, New Zealand
(a division of Pearson New Zealand Ltd.)
Penguin Books (South Africa) (Pty.) Ltd., 24 Sturdee Avenue,
Rosebank, Johannesburg 2196, South Africa

Penguin Books Ltd., Registered Offices: 80 Strand, London WC2R 0RL, England

Strawberry Shortcake™ and related trademarks © 2012 Those Characters From Cleveland, Inc. Used under license by Penguin Young Readers Group. First published in 2010 by Grosset & Dunlap, an imprint of Penguin Group (USA) Inc. Published in 2012 by Penguin Young Readers, an imprint of Penguin Group (USA) Inc., 345 Hudson Street, New York, New York 10014. Manufactured in China.

Library of Congress Control Number: 2009021136

ISBN 978-0-448-45345-3   10 9 8 7 6 5 4 3

A Picnic
Adventure

by Lisa Gallo
illustrated by Laura Thomas

Penguin Young Readers
An Imprint of Penguin Group (USA) Inc.

It is berry nice outside!

Strawberry Shortcake
and her friends will
go on a hike.

Blueberry Muffin
tells her friends about
Berry Bitty Falls.

They can have
a picnic there!

7

The girls pack
a yummy lunch.

8

Blueberry takes a map.

Orange Blossom brings a camera.

On the hike, Lemon Meringue
sees a rosebush.

Orange takes a photo.

Say cheese!

Look!

A cool stream.

Orange takes a photo.

Click!

Strawberry picks up

some rocks.

Then, Plum Pudding

sees a bird's nest.

Orange takes a photo.

Blueberry looks at the map.

They are berry close
to the waterfall!

They find the waterfall!

It is berry pretty!

The girls sit down.

They have a picnic.

19

Now it is time to go home.

They take one last photo.

Oh no!

The map blew away!

Blueberry is scared.

24

How will they get home

without the map?

Strawberry has an idea!

They will get home

if they find the nest,

the stream, and the roses.

Where is the bird's nest?

There it is!

Where is the stream?

There it is!

The girls are going the right way.

Hooray!

Where is the rosebush?

There it is!

The girls are almost home!

Look, the café!

They made it home.

What a great day!